MY BIG BOOK
OF ADVENTURES

Bath • New York • Singapore • Hong Kong • Cologne • Delhi
Melbourne • Amsterdam • Johannesburg • Auckland • Shenzhen

This edition published by Parragon in 2011
Parragon
Queen Street House
4 Queen Street
Bath BA1 1HE, UK

Base on the 'Winnie the Pooh' works, by A.A. Milne and E.H. Shepard

ISBN 978-1-4454-5219-7

Printed in China

Contents

Winnie the Pooh's Easter 9

Winnie the Pooh's Christmas 31

Winnie the Pooh's Valentine 69

Winnie the Pooh's April Fools' Day 89

Winnie the Pooh's Halloween 119

Winnie the Pooh and the Blustery Day 149

Winnie the Pooh and a Day for Eeyore 195

Winnie the Pooh's Easter

W innie the Pooh felt so happy to see the Hundred-Acre Wood in all its new spring finery. The magic of the season was shaking off the sleep of winter, so Pooh was climbing the path that led to a very special place called "Up There."

In the middle of the clearing Up There, perched on its large end, sat the biggest egg Pooh had ever seen!

My, thought Pooh, that egg is as tall as Christopher Robin. Perhaps taller!

Its size, however, wasn't the most surprising thing about the egg. It was all violet stripes and bright green squiggles, yellow polka dots and pink swirls!

Pooh laughed out loud. Pooh's very good friends heard him

laugh, and came to find out just what was so funny.

"Oh, my goodness," squeaked an amazed Piglet. "That is the most un-very-small egg I have ever seen!"

Gopher squinted and surveyed the egg carefully. "That's some breakfast!"

"This is nothin'," chuckled Tigger. "But I'll bet the look on the chicken's face was something to see! Hoo-hoo-hoo!"

"Oh, don't be silly," snapped Rabbit. "It's obvious this egg has

nothing to do with chickens or breakfasts!"

"Obvious to whom?" rumbled Eeyore. "If you don't mind my asking."

"You mean to tell me none of you knows what sort of egg this is?" demanded Rabbit.

"Well," hooted Owl, "it's not an owl egg. I can say that with certainty and not a small amount of relief."

"It's an Easter egg!" Rabbit announced triumphantly.

There was silence as everyone digested this revelation.

"Don't you know?" asked Rabbit. "Easter is a holiday, and

it's now! This is the time of year everyone gives decorated eggs to one another. I have it on very good authority from my distant cousin, who is a personal acquaintance of someone who knows the Easter Bunny's gardener!"

"Ah!" replied Pooh.

"Why," muttered Eeyore, "would anyone do a thing like that?"

"Well," Rabbit answered, "it seems, at least from what I've been told, that these are very special eggs."

"Very special how, bunny boy?" Tigger wanted to know.

"It appears," Rabbit said, "that they can talk."

"Ah!" Pooh said again.

"To be specific," Rabbit sniffed importantly, "they are supposed to say how very much we care for one another."

"Hmph," said Gopher, "I'll bet this egg says it loud!"

They all gathered close around the egg and listened carefully.

"It's not saying anything now," said Tigger.

"P-perhaps it's shy," said Piglet, giving the egg a gentle pat. "I imagine that it feels quite out of place."

"Perhaps if we make it feel at home, it'll feel more like talking," Pooh cried.

"But how does one make an egg feel at home?" asked Rabbit.

Pooh smiled. "I believe I have an idea."

It seemed as if no time had passed at all before Pooh's plan was put into effect. It appeared as if the giant egg was no longer the only Easter egg Up There.

Pooh had painted himself a bubbly pink with baby-blue
freckles. Tigger had acquired a checkerboard pattern of pastels.
Piglet was very red, while Owl was sky blue. Gopher had
become yellow and Eeyore now had lavender polka dots.

"It has to speak sooner or later, doesn't it?" sighed Pooh.
"I mean, if it's going to say it cares and all?"

"Maybe we have to tell it how much we care first,"
suggested Eeyore.

19

"How do we do that?" asked Piglet.

"The only proper way to speak to an egg," Owl informed everyone, "is when you are sitting on it."

"But," said Tigger, "I wouldn't want anyone sitting on me unless I was pretty sure he knew what he was doing!"

Everyone began rubbing their chins and scratching their heads, furiously trying to figure out what they were going to do.

Then Rabbit put his arm around Pooh's shoulders. "This time I have a plan, Pooh Bear."

"Ah!" said Pooh.

The next thing Pooh knew, Tigger was standing on top of

the egg, tugging on Pooh's paws, while Rabbit stood beneath
and pushed for all he was worth. But before anyone could
get Pooh seated, let alone ask the egg anything, away it went,
rolling down the hill, its bright colours shifting like a windmill!

They chased the rolling egg downhill and up...
through rushing streams and muddy spaces...
across wide meadows...
under bridges...

...and over valleys until...
the egg rolled to a halt, spinning
around on its side, turning more and
more slowly until finally it stopped...
with its tip pointing directly at
Christopher Robin!

"What are you doing with my
Easter egg?" he asked.

"Delivering it?" Pooh suggested
with a smile.

"Well, actually," said Christopher Robin, "this is your egg. All of yours!"

"So when is it going to tell us how much it cares?" Eeyore demanded.

Christopher Robin said, "Watch." He grasped the huge egg and began to twist the top. The egg slowly began to unscrew!

In a moment, Christopher Robin removed the top half of the egg and lifted out another egg painted to look very much like Winnie the Pooh!

One after another, each a bit smaller than the last, an egg in the image of each of Christopher Robin's friends was revealed.

"I'm going to keep mine next to my bedside table," decided Pooh.

"Isn't that a strange place for an Easter egg?" asked Christopher Robin.

"Oh, my goodness, not at all," chuckled Pooh. "Then the last thing it tells me before I fall asleep at night and the first thing it says when I open my eyes in the morning will be how very much somebody cares."

"Happy Easter, silly old bear!"

Winnie
the Pooh's
Christmas

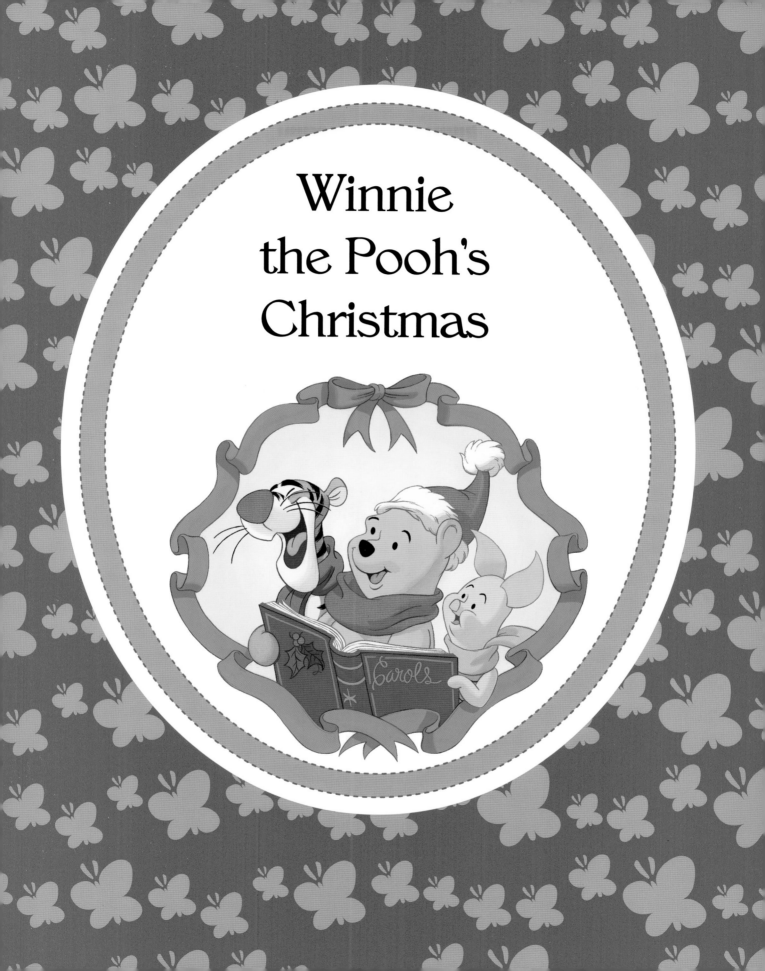

It was the night before Christmas, and Winnie the Pooh's nose was pressed flat against a windowpane. He was gazing out at the snowflakes hushing the Hundred-Acre Wood, gathering cosily like bedclothes around the house where he lived.

"I'm very glad to see you," Pooh chuckled to the plump snowflakes drifting past. "You're just in time for Christmas, which, if you must be in time for something, is something very nice to be in time for!"

Pooh turned to take a look at his house full of decorations. "Let me see, a tree, some candles..." He scratched his head and sighed. "There seems to be something...missing!"

All at once Pooh heard a rattle of very small knocks at his
front door. "Perhaps," Pooh smiled to himself, "that is whatever
it is that's missing!"

Pooh opened the door to find a very small snowman with a
pair of very Piglet-looking ears.

"Oh!" remarked Pooh, who was a very surprised bear. Then he added "Hello!" to be polite, because one should always be polite, even to surprises.

"H-h-hello, P-Pooh B-Bear," the snowman answered in a very Piglet-sounding voice. "M-Merry Christmas!"

Pooh wondered whether it was more polite to invite the snowman in where it was warm or let him stay outside where snowmen are usually more comfortable. The snowman finally gave Pooh a very small hint. "May I come in?" it asked.

"Please do," said Pooh.

The snowman hurried inside and stood before the fireplace. "The only thing I don't like about Christmas," said the snowman, "and it's a very small thing, is that my ears get so very cold."

"I can imagine," replied Pooh, who could not imagine a snowman's ears being anything but cold.

The snowman stood shivering in front of the fire and, with every tremble and quiver, began to look less and less like a snowman and more and more like Piglet.

"Why, hello, Piglet!" blurted Pooh, delighted to see his very best friend standing in a puddle of water. "If I had known it was you, I would have invited you in!"

Piglet smiled up at his friend. "Oh, Pooh! You did invite me in! You knew it was me all along."

"Well, of course I did, Piglet," responded Pooh.

"My!" breathed Piglet in wonder as he gazed up at Pooh's Christmas tree. "I've never seen so many candles on one tree."

"Well," explained Pooh, "there seemed to be a great many empty honeypots to use for candleholders. And there was a great deal of extra room on the tree because the popcorn didn't seem to get strung."

"Would you like me to help you string the popcorn, Pooh?" Piglet asked.

"Why, yes, Piglet. I'd like that very much,"answered
Pooh. "That is, if there were any popcorn left to string,
which there isn't."

"Oh, dear," said Piglet. He looked around nervously,
leaned close to Pooh, and whispered, "What happened to
it all?"

"I ate it," Pooh whispered back. "I was tasting it to make sure it was properly popped, and by the time I was sure" – Pooh shrugged and sighed – "it was all gone. I do, however, still have the string."

"That's all right, Pooh!" Piglet laughed. "We can use the string to wrap your gifts!"

"But, Piglet," chuckled Pooh, "the gifts won't be here until tomorrow morning. And then I unwrap them."

Pooh leaned close and whispered confidentially into Piglet's ear. "That's the way it's done, you know."

There may have been a few things about Christmas on which Pooh was a little hazy, but opening presents wasn't one of them.

"No, Pooh, I mean I'll help you wrap the presents you're going to give!"

Pooh's smile disappeared. "Oh!" he said quietly. "Those gifts." Then even more quietly, he added, "Oh, bother!"

"What's the matter, Pooh?" Piglet asked.

Pooh sighed tremendously. "I think I just remembered
what I forgot," he said. "It's presents."

"No presents?" Piglet looked up at Pooh sadly. "Not
even a very small one?"

Pooh shook his head. "I'm sorry, Piglet."

Piglet smiled bravely. "It's all right, Pooh. I always get a bit too excited opening presents. And it's the thought that counts, you know," he sniffed. "I think I'll take my very cold ears and go home."

Pooh saw his friend to the door and watched him walk sadly down the path as the snowflakes began turning him into a very small snowman once again.

"Oh, my," Pooh said to himself as he wound his

scarf around his neck and stepped out into the snow. "If it's the thought that counts at Christmas, I think I'd better ask Christopher Robin what he thinks about thoughts and presents and Christmas and everything."

It was a long, chilly walk through the swirling night. The snowflakes tickled Pooh's nose and crept down the back

of his neck. He was very glad when he arrived at Christopher
Robin's house, and he knocked loudly on the door.

"Pooh Bear!" Christopher Robin exclaimed. "What a
wonderful surprise! Come in!"

Pooh was led into Christopher Robin's toasty den, ablaze
with lights and colours dancing merrily from candles to glass
balls to tinsel and back again!

"My!" Pooh breathed. "This certainly looks like Christmas!"

"So I suppose I can ask you what I came to find out" – he rubbed his chin thoughtfully – "as soon as I remember what it is."

But then Pooh stepped up to Christopher Robin's fireplace, where a row of socks of all shapes and sizes hung neatly from the mantelpiece.

"Don't you think," Pooh remarked, "that Christmas is, perhaps, not the best time for drying your washing?"

"Silly old bear," Christopher Robin laughed, ruffling the fluff on Pooh's head. "That's not washing. They're stockings to hold Christmas presents!"

"You mean," Pooh answered slowly, "you have to have stockings to put presents in?"

"Yes," said Christopher Robin, "that's the way it's done."

"Oh, bother!" said Pooh, looking down at his feet. Not only did he have no presents for his friends, but they had no stockings to put the presents in! Pooh, being a bear, had little use for stockings. All his friends in the Hundred-Acre Wood were much the same way.

When Pooh mentioned this, Christopher Robin laughed. "Come with me, Pooh Bear. I have plenty of stockings for everyone."

Christopher Robin showed Pooh a drawer containing socks and stockings of every size, shape and colour.

"These are all stockings who have lost their mates and would love to have someone with whom to share Christmas," said Christopher Robin. He scratched one of Pooh's ears. "It's the thought that counts, you know."

"Why, yes," replied Pooh, happy that Christopher Robin had remembered to answer the question that he had forgotten to ask. "Thank you very much, Christopher Robin."

Soon Pooh was walking happily home with his arms full of stockings. The snow had stopped falling, leaving a wonderful white blanket over the entire forest. It was as if the Hundred-Acre Wood had decorated itself for Christmas. A huge moon made it seem as bright as day.

"But," Pooh reminded himself with a yawn, "it is very late, and I must get these stockings delivered." He thought for a moment. "I must get everyone presents, too, of course, but the stockings come first."

And so Pooh, being as quiet as the soft night around him, crept into his friends' homes one by one, and left a stocking with a little note "From Pooh" hanging from each one's mantelpiece.

First, of course,
there was Piglet's house,
where Pooh placed a
very small stocking.

He then left a
striped one for Tigger
because he was sure
that was the sort of
stocking Tiggers like
best.

54

Pooh left a very
bright orange one at
Rabbit's house.

Eeyore got
the warmest and
friendliest stocking
Pooh could find.

Gopher received a
long, dark stocking.
Pooh thought it was
what a tunnel would
look like if a tunnel
was a stocking.

Finally,
Owl was given
a stocking the
colour of the
sky – in which,
Pooh thought, he
would like to fly
if he was Owl.

It was very, very late when Pooh nailed his own honey-coloured stocking to his very own mantelpiece.

"Now that this stocking business is all taken care of," said Pooh, settling down in his softest armchair, "I simply must do some serious thinking about what I am going to give my friends for Christmas." Pooh closed his eyes, and soon neither his snoring nor the sun rising over the Hundred-Acre Wood disturbed his thoughts.

In fact, Pooh did not stop his deep thinking – or loud
snoring – until a knock sounded at his door, accompanied
by a chorus of "Merry Christmas, Pooh Bear!"

Pooh opened his eyes and glanced about anxiously.

"Oh, no," he thought. "My friends are here for Christmas and I have no presents for any of them!"

"There's only one thing to do," he told himself sternly. "I shall simply have to tell my friends I'm sorry, but I only thought about presents for them."

Pooh opened his door and started to apologize, but before he could say a word, in rushed all his friends – Piglet, Tigger, Rabbit, Gopher, Eeyore and Owl – all thanking Pooh at once for his thoughtful gifts.

Piglet was wearing a new stocking hat. "My ears are very grateful, Pooh Bear. It was exactly what I wanted."

Tigger told Pooh how much he loved his new stripedy
sleeping bag. "It's cosier than cosy!"

Rabbit couldn't wait to tell how he'd always dreamed of
owning a colour-coordinated carrot cover. How could Pooh
possibly have known?

Gopher appreciated the 'bag' for carrying around his rock samples. "Never had one big enough before!"

Eeyore explained – if anyone was interested – that his tail
had never been warmer than it was in its new warmer.

Owl was positive his brand-new 'wind sock' would provide him with all the necessary data required to prevent the occasional crash landing through his dining room window!

Pooh put his hands behind his back and looked thoughtful. "Something awfully nice is going on, though I'm not at all sure how it happened."

"I'll tell ya how it happened, buddy bear," exclaimed Tigger. "It's called Christmas!" He shoved a large pot of honey, with a stripedy ribbon and bow, down the stocking hanging from Pooh's mantelpiece. The others quickly followed suit with presents of their own for Pooh, which all turned out to be pots of honey. What else would a Pooh Bear want for Christmas... or any other time?

"Christmas," sighed Pooh happily. "What a very sweet thought, indeed!"

Winnie the Pooh's Valentine

It was easy to see what day it was in the Hundred-Acre Wood. Birds cuddled in pairs on drooping limbs and were loudly chirping duets. Friendly breezes tickled the leaves of trees until they fluttered with laughter. Saplings shyly touched and, bending close, exchanged sweet secrets in restless whispers. It always seemed, on Valentine's Day, that things were more tightly wrapped around each other than usual.

At Winnie the Pooh's house, things were taking on a decidedly "heartfelt" appearance, mostly because Pooh had just finished tacking up his "felt hearts" in all the most strategic places. Strategic, Owl had once explained, meant the places where things were sure to be in the way and, therefore, attract the most attention.

Pooh's happy contemplation of his handiwork was suddenly interrupted by a quiet voice saying "Pooh Bear" in a most polite tone.

Startled, Pooh turned so quickly he bumped his nose on a

felt heart stuck to the back of a very hard door.

"Oh, bother!" sniffed Pooh, as he noticed Roo standing anxiously in the middle of his parlour floor. "Why, hello, little Roo!" he exclaimed.

"Hello, Pooh," responded Roo. "Is that felt?" he asked, pointing to the heart.

Pooh cautiously rubbed his nose. "Oh, I felt it, all right," he assured Roo woefully.

"No," said Roo, "is that heart felt?"

"Oh!" said Pooh, not really understanding the question. "No, I don't think the heart felt it at all."

Roo smiled brightly at the bear of very little brain and knew that it was time to talk about something else. "Would you mind terribly," he asked politely, "if we talk about something besides your felt hearts?"

"That would be wonderful," breathed Pooh in relief. "What did you have in mind?"

"I want to give a valentine to my mum," Roo whispered, "but I don't know how."

"Neither do I!" laughed Pooh, who was always delighted to

73

agree with someone about something. But his laughter ceased as soon as he saw the look on little Roo's face.

"Then what'll I do?" piped Roo, feeling a distress so profound he could hardly keep his eyes from filling with tears.

"What we will do," said Pooh, taking Roo's hand in his own, "is find out how!"

In no time at all, Pooh and Roo had gathered together all

74

their best friends – Piglet, Tigger, Rabbit, Gopher and, of course, Eeyore – and put Roo's question to them.

"Well," suggested Piglet in a very small voice, "the most important thing about a valentine you give to someone is that it says 'I love you.'"

"Yeah!" agreed Tigger, bouncing around Pooh's parlour in excitement. "An' it's got to say it in bright colours!"

"Impressive!" whistled Gopher. "It's got to be impressive 'cause sayin' 'I love you' is a pretty impressive proposition."

"And because 'I love you' are the most important words one person can

75

say to another," sniffed Rabbit knowingly, "a valentine should say them in as many different ways as possible."

"What do you think, Eeyore?" Pooh asked the donkey, who was being even more silent than usual.

"Well, since you're askin'," rumbled Eeyore in his very slow way, "I suppose the sort of valentine you're plannin' is definitely one way of going about it."

"Then what're we waitin' for?" hooted Tigger. "Christmas?"

"I'll get my tools," said Gopher gleefully.

"I'll get my dictionary," said Rabbit.

"I'll clean up when we're through," said Piglet.

"And I'll tell you what I think of it when it's finished," announced Eeyore, "if anyone is interested, that is."

Gopher chiseled a huge heart out of a boulder he had been

saving for just such a special
occasion.

It was twice as tall as
Tigger balanced on the
very tip-top of his tail.

"Impressive," everyone
told Gopher when he
was done.

The irrepressible feline
wasted not a moment painting
the heart with the most spectacular
colours he could think of, bright orange
with black stripedy stripes,

"Posilutely
splendiferous," Tigger
purred when he'd
completed his task.

And as Piglet swept up the work area, Roo climbed up onto the obliging Eeyore's back and wrote "I love you" on the heart in his very best writing. Everyone agreed that although it was very small as writing goes, it couldn't have been more neatly done.

Then, after consulting a dictionary so thick he'd had to haul it all the way from his house in a wheelbarrow, Rabbit added a great many words and phrases, including "Kiss me goodnight" and "Do your homework" and "Eat your vegetables," as well as "Smoochface," "Pookums," and – Rabbit's personal favourite – "Snugglebunny."

The completed project was a magnificent, no, an impressive, sight. The friends were all quite pleased with themselves until Roo, after studying the valentine for some time, suddenly blurted out, "But how am I going to get this to my mother?"

Spirits plummeted. No one had thought of how this valentine was going to be delivered to Kanga. Mailing it was out of the question. Even if an envelope of the proper size could have been produced in time, the correct number of postage stamps would have weighed more than the valentine itself.

Sitting in a sad little circle, the friends were unable to come up with any helpful ideas at all.

"I guess we're finished," sighed Tigger hopelessly.

"Then now's the time I'll tell you what I thought," announced Eeyore, "if you really want to know, that is."

"Oh, I think we really do want to know, Eeyore," said Pooh.

"I think," said Eeyore, "what I thought all along. This valentine is definitely one way of doing it."

"Why, Eeyore!" exclaimed Pooh. "I believe that's very helpful!"

"It is?" brayed the startled donkey.

"Certainly," explained Pooh, furrowing his brow. "If this is one way of doing a valentine, that means there must be a two way!"

Everyone exchanged amazed smiles and nods as Roo leaped excitedly to his feet.

"You're right, Pooh! You're right!" he shouted. "And I know exactly what the two way is, thanks to all of you!"

That evening at just about supper-time (according to the rumblings of Pooh's tummy), they all watched as Roo presented his mother, Kanga, with a handful of beautiful wildflowers. "These flowers," Roo explained to Kanga, "say 'I love you' . . ."

Pooh poked Piglet to make sure he'd heard, but the smile on Piglet's face revealed that he hadn't missed a thing.

" . . . and," Roo continued, "they say it in very bright colours."

Tigger puffed out his chest so far he nearly fell off his tail.

"And because the flowers are all different kinds, they say 'I love you' in lots of different ways."

Rabbit remarked that he had something in his eye so no one should think he was crying or anything.

"And," said Roo, completing the presentation, "they're the most impressive valentine I could carry all by myself."

Gopher blew his nose into a brightly patterned bandanna.

"Thank you, Roo, dear," smiled Kanga. Sniffing the flowers, she added, "I couldn't have asked for a more perfect valentine."

As mother and son embraced, Tigger leaned over to Pooh and whispered, "But what'll we do with the valentine we made?"

"Keep it right where it is," Pooh whispered back. "It will remind us that there can be a lot of 'I love you' in every day if you know just where to look for it."

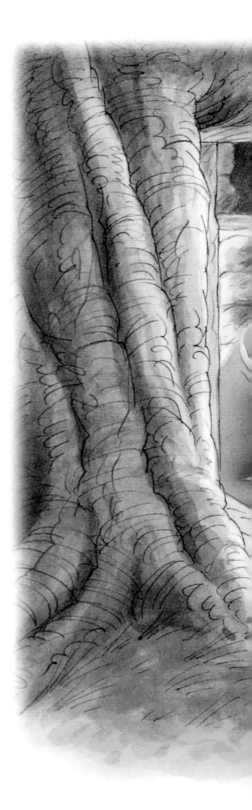

Winnie the Pooh's April Fools' Day

R abbit had called a meeting. Everyone in the Hundred-Acre Wood knew that Rabbit didn't call meetings unless something very significant was afoot. To Rabbit, meetings were as important as honey was to a certain bear of very short legs who was, at that very moment, stumping his way to Rabbit's as quickly as those same very short legs would allow.

Running just as quickly towards the meeting from a quite different direction (and on legs even shorter than Pooh Bear's) was Pooh's good friend Piglet.

And Eeyore, carrying his tail in his mouth so as not to lose it in his hurry, was galloping so rapidly to the gathering (from yet another direction) that his back legs would occasionally outdistance his front ones and the donkey would suddenly find

himself running backward. He would then have to stop and get himself sorted out before his frantic journey could continue.

Gopher was scurrying so rapidly through his tunnels in order to reach the meeting place on time that the trees above ground quaked gently as he jostled their roots in passing.

And high above those trembling treetops, Tigger tore

towards the meeting in a series of tremendous bounces.

Meanwhile, Rabbit, at whose house the meeting was to take place, couldn't contain his excitement and was scampering through the woods towards the others to make sure they were all on their way and would not be late.

As a result of this hurrying, scurrying, scampering, galloping, and bouncing, the friends not only were on time for the meeting but were even early! Everyone arrived at a particular crossroads at precisely the same moment, all moving too fast to stop until they'd tumbled head over heels over one another and

wound up in a friendly sort of tangle.

"I suppose," sniffed Rabbit after they all had untangled themselves, "that we can call the meeting to order right here and now so Pooh Bear can get on with his assignment."

Pooh's ears perked up in surprise. "As-SIGN-ment?! I'm not very good at making signs, you know. I'm never quite sure why using a certain letter isn't just as good as using one

of the others. It's quite confusing."

"This has nothing to do with making signs, Pooh Bear," Rabbit said. "It has to do with foolishness, which is why we need your help."

Rabbit looked down at Pooh and asked, "You do realize that today is April Fools' Day?"

"Of course," laughed Pooh, delighted to know the right answer for a change. "It's the one day of the year you can

look like a fool and not feel unhappy about it."

"Well, I suggest that this year we not be fooled," sniffed Rabbit, looking very determined.

"Might be nice for a change," said Tigger, with a grin. "We certainly do a stupenderous job o' looking pretty silly the entire rest o' the year."

"But today it's someone else's turn, by dinghy!" cackled Gopher.

"Really?" asked Pooh. "Whose turn is it?"

"I think Rabbit means he wants us to fool the April Fool before he fools us!" Piglet whispered into Pooh's ear.

Pooh leaned close to his friends and whispered, "How are we going to do it?"

Rabbit whispered back, "You're going to find the April Fool and bring him to my house."

"I am?" asked Pooh in amazement.

"But be careful, Pooh," warned Piglet. "I've heard that the April Fool can look like anybody!"

"He can?" gasped Pooh.

"Absolutely," whistled Gopher. "That's how he fools ya!"

"Don't worry, Pooh boy," Tigger assured Pooh with a slap on the back. "You'll find him. Nobody knows more about foolishness than you do."

As the others hurried off to Rabbit's house to prepare their surprise for the April Fool, Pooh scratched his head furiously with both hands. It didn't help. He hadn't the faintest idea of where to start looking for the April Fool – or what to do with him if he found him.

All at once Pooh recalled that fool rhymed with pool. He proceeded immediately to the largest collection of water in the forest – a quiet pond near the river. As Pooh cautiously crossed from one side of this pool to the other on a series of stepping-stones, the one that happened to be a turtle and not a rock tipped him headfirst into the water.

Sitting on the bottom of the pool, Pooh was, needless to say, thoroughly disappointed. There was not a single fool to be found.

So Pooh began to look in places that didn't rhyme with fool.

All he found in a cave were some pesky echoes that
loved to make fools of people but were not precisely
foolish themselves. They were not precisely anything,
really, except a lot of noise, and Pooh, who was very
well acquainted with the likes of Rabbit and Eeyore and
Owl, knew that a lot of noise didn't make one foolish . . .
most of the time. And the bats, that all this noise

awakened, hadn't any interest in fools, only in chasing
Pooh away so they could go back to sleep. Pooh
managed to escape by plunging back into the pool and
sitting on the bottom until the flying grumps returned to
their napping.

And when Pooh poked his nose into a certain large
hollow tree, he was suddenly swamped by an avalanche

of acorns left over from a squirrel's winter storage. Slipping and sliding, Pooh found himself sitting down hard in the pool once again.

Exhausted and quite damp, Pooh scrunched his face up into a painful frown. He was positive his friends were right in thinking that he could find the April Fool because foolishness was, after all, something with which he had a great deal of experience. Besides that, he couldn't remember his friends ever being wrong.

Pooh sighed and unscrewed his face. "Perhaps I should go

to Rabbit's house and ask for help," he said to himself. But he immediately shook his head. "No, that would be foolish. They're busy getting ready to fool the April Fool."

All at once Pooh sat up straight, and a smile lit up his face.

"If it's foolish to go to Rabbit's," Pooh exclaimed, "then that's where the April Fool will be!"

Without wasting another moment, Pooh set off as fast as his dripping legs could carry him.

At Rabbit's house, everyone was ready for the arrival of the April Fool.

Rabbit had set a huge
bucket of water over his
front door to spill onto the
Fool's head when he entered.

Piglet was nearby
with a very small, yet
very tasteful, cream
pie he'd made from his
favourite recipe to toss
into the Fool's face.

Off to one side stood Tigger
with a huge pepper shaker to
sprinkle on the Fool's nose and
make him sneeze.

The small rag rug in the entrance was clamped firmly in Eeyore's mouth to be yanked out from under the Fool's feet.

Finally, Gopher was prepared to spill a bag of fluffy feathers that would cling to the damp Fool and cause him to resemble a giant chicken.

The front door flew open, and there stood Winnie
the Pooh, shouting "April Fool!" at the top of his voice.

The horrified Rabbit tried to save Pooh from the
falling bucket of water but succeeded only in getting
it jammed over his own head, which caused him to
stumble about blindly.

He bumped into Tigger, who staggered backward

and sat in Piglet's pie, accidentally sprinkling his pepper into Eeyore's nose.

Eeyore, still hanging on to the rug, emitted such a powerful sneeze that it propelled him backward into Gopher, who spilled his feathers all over Piglet as the rug jerked out from under Pooh's feet and set the bear down in the entrance with a loud thump.

After a moment of shocked silence Pooh finally managed to blurt out, "The April Fool is here!" Then he looked down at his still-dripping jersey. "But he did seem to be very much out there, too."

Then the laughter began. And it was quite a while before anyone could speak.

Finally, Rabbit, wiping the tears of mirth from his eyes, put his arm around Pooh's shoulders and said, "I think you've discovered the Fool's secret, Pooh Bear!"

"I have?"

"It seems the April Fool," hooted Tigger, "looks just like us!"

"And a good thing, too," sighed Pooh.

"Why's that, Pooh Bear?" demanded Piglet, trying to

remove a particularly large feather from his very small ear.

"Because then we can all laugh with one another – and not at anyone," said Pooh. "Or am I being foolish?"

"No, Pooh," said Piglet with a smile. "Not this time."

And the laughter began again and went on and on for a very long time.

Winnie the Pooh's Halloween

The late afternoon sun appeared to hesitate on the horizon, settling comfortably among the tip-top branches of the trees in the Hundred-Acre Wood.

"Look," chuckled Winnie the Pooh from the grassy knoll where he and his friends were watching the sunset. "The sun doesn't want to go to bed!"

"Perhaps it's afraid of the dark," suggested Piglet, who was much fonder of the sun's arriving than he was of its going to bed.

Christopher Robin put his arm comfortingly around Piglet's shoulders. "No, Piglet," he explained, "the sun simply wants to stay and share Halloween with us."

"Oh?" remarked Pooh Bear, his tummy grumbling. "Is Halloween, perhaps, a very small smackeral of something sweet" – he licked his lips hopefully – "to eat?"

"Don't be silly, Pooh Bear," snorted Rabbit. "A Halloween isn't something to eat."

"'Course not," agreed Tigger, bouncing up and down on his coiled tail. "Everybody knows that."

"Pardon me for saying so," interrupted Eeyore, "but knowing what something *isn't* doesn't exactly tell us what something *is*, which seems to me to be the point, if that's what we're looking for. The point, I mean."

"Never mind the point," whistled Gopher. "All I want to know is what the ding-dang we're talking about!"

"Halloween," announced Pooh, proud of himself for remembering.

"And what exactly is a Halloween?" demanded Gopher.

The friends exchanged shrugs and puzzled frowns, then turned to Christopher Robin for an answer.

"Halloween," Christopher Robin informed them excitedly, "is the scariest holiday of the year – because it takes place at night."

"If you don't mind," responded Piglet, trying to keep his ears from trembling, "I think I'll be thinking as little as possible about scary things that happen in the dark."

"But that's what Halloween is," protested Christopher Robin. "When the sun goes down, we all dress up in costumes and see who can be the scariest."

Piglet noticed the sun was no longer resting comfortably in the treetops but was, in fact, almost out of sight behind the horizon.

"Uh, I'm sorry, but I won't have time to play Halloween with you," Piglet blurted out. "I have some very important things to do."

"What could be more important than scaring the pants off each other in the dark?" Tigger asked.

"Turning on every light in my house and dusting under my bed," said Piglet, hurrying away into the dusk.

"Poor Piglet," sighed Christopher Robin. "But I suppose the nice thing about a holiday is that we all have the opportunity to suit ourselves."

"And that's just what I'm going to do," laughed Tigger, bouncing around his friends in excited circles. "Suit myself up in the most fantastical costume I can think of! Hoo-hoo-HOO!"

As the others shouted their agreement, Pooh was strangely silent.

"What's the matter, Pooh Bear?" Christopher Robin asked as they all scattered to prepare their costumes.

"Well," Pooh responded, "I suppose I'm going to miss sharing Halloween with my best friend, Piglet."

"That is too bad," Christopher Robin agreed. "You're simply going to have to have twice as much fun as anyone else and share it with him later."

"Why, what a nice idea!" exclaimed Pooh. "And I'll have to be twice as scary, too."

"You'd better get started on your costume," laughed Christopher Robin.

"Oh, yes," Pooh mused. "My costume."

Pooh remembered that his scariest experiences were whenever he visited the honey tree for an extra smackeral before, or after, whatever meal it happened to be. (Eating always made Pooh very hungry.)

"Nothing is scarier than a honeybee," Pooh decided, "and that's what I'm going to be . . . a BEE!"

So when Pooh arrived home, he immediately opened up his chest of odds and ends of no possible use to anyone except to a bear of very little brain, and began to look for his costume.

In no time at all Pooh
was ready.
    With black paint,
Pooh had painted large
stripes around
his middle.

A plunger was stuck to
his sitting-down side (with
a small flag attached
proclaiming "Stinger"
in case anyone needed
reminding).

And on his head
were Pooh's answer to
antennae – two wobbly
springs capped with
Ping-Pong balls.

"Now, that,"
Pooh said to
himself as he
examined
his image in the
mirror, "is very
alarming indeed!"

He hurried out to meet his friends. No one would be better suited for Halloween than he.

The night had become quite dark. Pooh would have walked right over Gopher without seeing him, but then he noticed two glowing eyes peering out of the gloom.

"Well?" Gopher's voice demanded. "What do you think?"

Pooh had to look very closely to distinguish his practically invisible friend. He was wrapped head to foot in a billowing black cloak.

"Gopher!" Pooh exclaimed. "You certainly surprised me!"

"I knew I would," Gopher sniggered. "Nothing's spookier than a dark night, so that's what I decided to be. Scared myself out of a week's sleep when I looked in the mirror. Love this Halloween."

Before Pooh and Gopher could discuss costumes further, Tigger dropped very suddenly out of the night sky and landed between them. Then, with a loud "Hoo-hoo-HOO!" he squirted them both with a small water pistol.

"Tigger," spluttered Pooh, rubbing the water out of his eyes and gazing at his friend in wonder.

Tigger had donned a bright-red jersey emblazoned with a wriggly bolt of yellow lightning.

"Who are you?" whistled Gopher.

"You know the rainstorm everyone's so afraid is going to show up?" Tigger asked.

"Well, I'm here! Terrifryin', ain't I?"

"Not to me," rumbled a voice from behind them.

All three spun around in surprise. "Eeyore!" they shouted.

Eeyore was wearing a large red nose as well as a yellow ruffled collar around his neck. On his head was perched the pointiest clown hat anyone had ever seen crowned by a feathery orange ball.

"I was afraid if I were too frightening, I'd have to spend Halloween alone," Eeyore explained. "Hope I didn't frighten anyone too badly."

Pooh reassured him. "If I hadn't heard your friendly voice first, I'm sure I would be running for my life this very moment."

"I shouldn't believe you," grumbled Eeyore. Then a smile spread over his face. "But I'm going to because it feels so good."

136

The four friends began a long, loud laugh that stopped very suddenly when they saw Rabbit staring at them in annoyance.

"What are you laughing at?" Rabbit wanted to know. "This is the most frightening costume I could think of."

Rabbit had pasted soft clumps of white cotton all over himself.

"Perhaps it would be more frightening," suggested Eeyore gently, "if you told us what you are."

Rabbit leaned close and whispered, "A dust bunny!" and shuddered at the thought. "There's nothing more frightening to me than those little balls of fluff with minds of their own collecting where I can't take a broom to them!"

The thought of wayward dust suddenly reminded Pooh of Piglet huddled alone under his bed.

"I'm sure Piglet would be terrified of your costume, Rabbit," said Pooh sadly.

Before Rabbit could respond, however, a long, low moan sounded, rattling ominously out of the darkness, causing everyone to stiffen in surprise.

"Woooooooooooooooooo!"

"What was that?" Tigger whispered.

"I don't think I want to wait to see this costume," said Rabbit with a shiver.

"Woooooooooooooooooo!"

Another moan drifted out of the blackness under the trees.

"I think we should go to Piglet's," suggested Pooh, "and make sure he's not too frightened."

"You're right, Pooh. That's what friends are for. Last one to Piglet's house is . . . not first!" shouted Tigger.

The friends ran headlong through the Hundred-Acre Wood. In the distance Piglet's house had every light ablaze and shone like a beacon to guide weary travellers home.

Tigger threw open Piglet's front door and sped inside, followed closely by Rabbit, Gopher and Pooh, with a panting Eeyore bringing up the rear.

Thundering across Piglet's gleaming floor, they all tried to stop, but the hours of careful waxing proved their downfall.

Skidding through the house, they all slipped onto their soft sides and slid in a tangle to end up in a pile under Piglet's bed!

"Piglet?" Pooh called out.

"Woooooooooooooooooo!" sounded the answer.

"It got Piglet," Pooh whispered.

"No," answered Piglet. Then the bedspread lifted, and Piglet joined them under the bed. "It didn't get me. It IS me!"

"Who would have guessed," Pooh laughed, "that the scariest costume turned out to be no costume at all?"

"You see," Piglet explained, "I was so scared about being scared that I knew the only way Halloween was going to be a holiday for me was if I was the most frightening one of all!"

"And you did a stupendous job," laughed Tigger, patting Piglet on the back. "But what do we do now?"

"Well," said Pooh thoughtfully. "Why don't we stay here and share Halloween?"

"And have hot chocolate," suggested Eeyore.

"And tell scary stories," added Tigger.

"Excellent!" announced Rabbit. "I'll go first. Once upon a time, there was a giant dust bunny. . . ."

As Rabbit continued, Pooh put his arm around Piglet's shoulders.

"I think I like Halloween, Pooh Bear," Piglet whispered to his friend.

"Me, too, Piglet," Pooh whispered back as he scooted closer. "Me, too!"

Winnie
the Pooh
and the Blustery Day

One fine day, the East Wind traded places with the West Wind, and that stirred things up a bit in the Hundred-Acre Wood.

And on that windy day, Winnie the Pooh decided to visit his Thoughtful Spot. As he walked along, he made up a little hum. This is how it went:

> Oh, the wind is lashing lustily,
> and the trees are thrashing thrustily,
> and the leaves are rustling gustily,
> so it feels that it will undoubtedly be . . .
> a rather blustery day!

As soon as Pooh reached his Thoughtful Spot, he sat right down and tried to think of something.

"Think, think, think, think, think," Pooh mumbled to himself. But nothing came to mind.

"Think, think, think," Pooh tried again, putting one paw to his head as if to catch any stray thoughts that might come wandering along.

Suddenly Gopher popped out of his gopher hole and said, "What's wrong, sonny? Got yourself a headache?"

"No," Pooh replied. "I was just thinking."

"Is that so?" said Gopher. "Well, if I were you, I'd think about skedaddling out of here. It's Windsday, you know."

"Windsday? Why, so it is," said Pooh. And then he finally had a thought – and it was a good one, at that. "I think I shall go wish everyone a happy Windsday," Pooh announced. "And I shall begin with my very dear friend Piglet."

Piglet lived in the middle of the forest in a very grand house.
And on this blustery day, he was sweeping the fallen leaves away
from his front door. He had just swept the last leaf away when a
big gust of wind blew it right back at him, scooping him up and
whisking him away. "I don't mind the leaves that are leaving . . . ,"
Piglet observed. "It's the leaves that are coming." And with that, he
was blown right into Pooh Bear.

"Happy Windsday," said Pooh as another great gust of wind lifted Piglet right off his little pink feet.

"Well, it isn't very happy for me," Piglet said with a gulp.

"Where are you going?" Pooh cried, running after his friend.

"That's what I'm asking myself," Piglet said. "Where . . . ?"

"And what do you think you will answer yourself?" Pooh asked, grabbing hold of Piglet's scarf just before he floated out of reach.

"Oh, Pooh, I'm unravelling!" Piglet cried.

Indeed he was. Or rather, his scarf was. Like a pink kite on a long green string, Piglet went sailing off into the sky.

"Oh dear. Oh d-d-d-dear, dear," he stammered, clutching onto the string.

"Hang on, Piglet," cried Pooh from down below.

It wasn't long before Piglet was flying over Kanga's house. Kanga had just hopped outside to get the post.

"Look, Mama," said Roo, peering out of his mother's pouch. "A kite!"

"That's not a kite," said Kanga. "It's Piglet!"

And before Kanga could say another word, Pooh skidded to a stop in front of her. "Happy Windsday, Kanga," he said. "Happy Windsday, Roo."

"Can I fly Piglet next, Pooh?" Roo asked.

But Pooh and Piglet had already breezed past little Roo.

"Oh dear, oh dear, oh-dear-oh-dear-oh-dear," cried Piglet as he swooped right and left in the gusty air.

"Oh bo-bo-bother," Pooh exclaimed, bouncing and sliding along below him.

When Piglet finally found the nerve to look down, there was Eeyore, looking up at him. Eeyore was busy repairing his house, which the wind had blown to pieces. He had just put the last stick back in place when Pooh came crashing through.

"Happy Windsday, Eeyore," said Pooh. Then he went zipping off again, still holding on to the remains of Piglet's scarf.

"Thanks for noticin' me," said Eeyore.

Not far from Eeyore's house was Rabbit's garden.

"Ah, what a refreshing day for harvesting," Rabbit said aloud as he pulled up a large orange carrot.

Looking up, he suddenly saw Pooh coming towards him at top speed.

"Oh no!" shouted Rabbit, waving his arms frantically.

"Happy Windsday," Pooh called, kicking up a whole row of carrots.

"Oh, *yes*!" Rabbit chuckled as the juicy, ripe carrots fell smack into his wheelbarrow.

Stronger and stronger the West Wind blew. And before long, Piglet found himself blown right up against Owl's window.

Owl was awakened from a peaceful snooze by the loud crash. "Whoo?" he said, opening his big round eyes. "Who is it?"

"It's me," Piglet said. "P-p-p-please, may I come in?"

"Well, I say now," Owl said, his eyes rounder than ever. "Someone has pasted Piglet on my window."

Just then Pooh's face appeared beside Piglet's, and Owl invited them both in. Soon Pooh and Piglet were comfortably seated in Owl's cosy living room. "Am I correct in assuming that it's a rather blustery day?" asked Owl.

"Oh, yes. That reminds me. Happy Windsday, Owl," said Pooh, hungrily eyeing a big honeypot in front of him on the table.

"Windsday?" Owl hooted as the wind whistled through his house. "My good fellow, I wouldn't go so far as to call it Windsday. Just a mild zephyr."

"Excuse me, Owl, but is there any honey in that pot?" Pooh shouted over the howling wind.

"Oh, yes, of course," Owl said. "Help yourself." While Pooh eagerly reached for the pot of honey – which the wind had just blown clear across the table – Owl continued with his story.

"As I was saying, this is just a mild zephyr compared to the
big wind of sixty-seven. Or was it seventy-six?" Owl muttered,
scratching his head. "Oh well, no matter. I remember the big blow
well. It was the year my aunt Clara went to visit her cousin. Now,
her cousin was not only gifted on the glockenspiel, but . . . . "

And with the wild wind roaring through his house, Owl proceeded to tell his friends all about his aunt Clara's cousin. He didn't seem to notice when the teacups clattered to the floor. And he barely paused when the wind swept Piglet right out the door and back in again. It wasn't until the whole house came crashing down upon his ears that Owl finally finished his tale.

As soon as Christopher Robin heard the news, he hurried to the scene of Owl's disaster.

"What a pity," said Christopher Robin when he saw the state Owl's house was in. "I don't think we will ever be able to fix it."

"If you ask me," said Eeyore, "when a house looks like that, it's time to find another one." Then he shook his head and said, "It might take a day or two, but don't worry, Owl – I'll find you a new one."

"Good," said Owl, settling back in his rocking chair. "That will just give me time to tell you about my uncle Clyde. . . ."

And that's just what he did. On and on Owl talked until the blustery day turned into a blustery night.

166

For Pooh it turned out to be an anxious sort
of night, filled with anxious sorts of noises.

One was a particular noise he'd never heard
before:

"Rrrrrr!"

It wasn't a rumble. It wasn't a grumble.
And it wasn't exactly a growl. But whatever
it was, it was coming from just outside
Pooh's door.

"Is that you, Piglet?" Pooh called, but no one answered.
"Eeyore?" Pooh tried again. And finally, "Christopher Robin?"

When there was still no answer, Pooh got out of bed and went to
investigate. And being a bear of very little brain, he decided to invite
the new sound in.

"Hello?" he said, flinging the front door open.

Suddenly a big, bouncy creature bounded in and knocked Pooh flat on his back.

"*Rrrrrrr.* Hello," the creature said from atop Pooh's chest. "I'm Tigger."

"Oh," Pooh replied, looking up into Tigger's smiling face. "You scared me."

"Sure I did," Tigger said good-naturedly. "Everyone's scared of Tiggers. Who are you?"

"I'm Pooh," said Pooh.

"Ah, what's a Pooh?" Tigger asked.

"You're sitting on one," Pooh informed him.

And with no further ado, Tigger climbed off Pooh, stuck out his paw, and said, "Glad to meet ya. Tigger's my name. T-I–double Guh–Er. That spells Tigger!"

"But what's a Tigger?" Pooh asked, plainly puzzled.

Without a pause, Tigger proudly replied:

> *The wonderful thing about Tiggers*
>> *is Tiggers are wonderful things.*
> *Their tops are made out of rubber,*
>> *and their bottoms are made of springs.*
> *They're bouncy, trouncy, flouncy, pouncy,*
>> *fun, fun, fun, fun, fun.*
> *But the most wonderful thing about Tiggers*
>> *is that I'm the only one!*

And to prove his point, Tigger bounced around the room on his springy tail repeating: "I'm the only one!"

"If you're the only one, what's that over there?" Pooh asked, pointing at Tigger's reflection in the mirror.

"What a strange-looking creature!" said Tigger. "Look at the beady little eyes, pur-posti-rus chin and ricky-diculus striped pyjamas!"

Pooh nodded, and then he said, "Looks like another Tigger to me."

Tigger decided to change the subject. "Ah, well, did I say I was hungry?"

"I don't think so," said Pooh.

"Well, then, I'll say it," said Tigger. "I'm hungry."

"Not for honey, I hope," Pooh said, casting a worried glance at his honeypot.

"Oh boy, honey!" Tigger cried. "That's what Tiggers like best."

"I was afraid of that," Pooh said as Tigger plopped down at the table, grabbed the honey, and dug his paw in.

"*Yum,*" Tigger said, putting a glob of honey in his mouth. "*Yuck!*" he said when he swallowed his first mouthful.

"Tiggers *don't* like honey," he gagged. "That sticky stuff is only fit for heffalumps and woozles."

"You mean elephants and weasels," Pooh corrected him.

"That's what I said. Heffalumps and woozles," Tigger said.

"Well, what do heff . . . ah . . . ah . . . hallalaff, ah . . . what do they do?" Pooh inquired.

"Oh, nothin' much," Tigger said nonchalantly. "Just steal honey." And with that, he went bouncing out the door and into the night.

Suddenly Pooh was all alone . . . Or was he?

Pooh had a horrible feeling that at least one heffalump – or was it a woozle? – was lurking about outside. So he bolted the door and picked up his pop gun, determined to stand guard over his honey.

Hour after hour, Pooh kept his lonely vigil while the very blustery night turned into a very rainy night. Lightning flashed. Thunder crashed. And somewhere between the flashing and crashing, Pooh fell asleep.

Pooh dreamed he was surrounded by heffalumps and woozles of all shapes and sizes. Some were black, and some were brown. Some were up, and some were down. Some had polka dots. Some had stripes. But they all had one thing in common: *they all wanted to steal his honey!*

As Pooh tightly clutched his honeypot, one of the heffalumps turned into a watering can and began dousing him with water. The chilly drops cascaded over Pooh, soaking him from head to toe.

He woke up suddenly, and the heffalumps and woozles were gone. But the water remained. It was already up to Pooh's knees, and more was leaking in through the ceiling.

Pooh slogged across the flooded floor to his mirror. After studying the very damp bear reflected there, he asked, "Is it raining where you are?" And without even waiting for an answer, he said, "It's raining where I am, too."

As a matter of fact, it was raining all over the Hundred-Acre Wood. The rain came down, down, down and the river rose up, up, up, rising so high it finally crept out of its bed and into Piglet's.

Poor Piglet was terrified. With the water swirling around him, he grabbed paper and pen and frantically scribbled: HELP! P . . . P . . . PIGLET. (ME.) Then he placed the message in a bottle and tossed it out his window and into the raging river.

As the rain came down, Piglet tried to scoop it up into a big iron pot. But the pot was not – most definitely not! – big enough for all that water.

Floating on top of a wooden chair, Piglet kept on bailing, but as he was bailing, he went sailing through the door.

Meanwhile, Pooh was having quite a difficult time himself. He had managed to save ten honeypots, and he sat with them on the branch of a tree, high above the river. More than ready for his supper, he stuck his head into one of the pots. But as Pooh tried to sop up his supper, the river sopped up Pooh, for he fell off the branch and into the swirling water below. Upside down, with his head still stuck in the honeypot, Pooh was carried along with the current.

The Hundred-Acre Wood got floodier and floodier. But the water couldn't come all the way up to Christopher Robin's house, so that's where everyone gathered. Everyone except Piglet, Pooh and Eeyore, that is.

In the midst of all the excitement, Eeyore stubbornly stuck to his task of finding a new home for Owl.

While Eeyore was off house-hunting, Roo made an important discovery. "Look!" he said. "I've found a bottle, and it's got something in it, too."

"It's a message," Christopher Robin declared. "It says: 'Help! P . . . P . . . Piglet. (Me.)'"

Turning to Owl, he said, "You must fly over to Piglet's house and tell him we'll make a rescue."

So Owl flew out over the flood, and soon he spotted two small objects below him.

One was little Piglet, caught in a whirlpool. And the other was Pooh, floating downstream, his head still stuck in the honeypot.

"Oh, Owl," Piglet said. "I don't mean to c-c-complain, but I'm so s-s-scared."

"Be brave, little Piglet," Owl advised. "Chin up and all that sort of thing."

"It's awfully hard to be b-b-brave when you're such a s-s-small animal," Piglet pointed out.

"Then to divert your small mind from your unfortunate predicament, I shall tell you an amusing anecdote," Owl offered. "It concerns a distant cousin of mine. . . ."

Owl had just begun his story when Piglet cried, "I beg your pardon, Owl, but I think we're coming to a flutterfall, a falatterfall, a very big w-waterfall!"

"Please," said Owl, holding up a warning wing. "No interruptions."

But Piglet was already being carried away by the current. A moment later he fell over the falls, with Pooh Bear close behind.

Head over heels the two friends tumbled down the rushing, gushing waterfall – down, down, down until they finally landed in a quiet pool far, far, far below.

"Oh, there you are, Pooh Bear," Owl said as Pooh popped up on Piglet's chair. "Now, to continue my story. . ."

Fortunately for Pooh, Owl didn't have time to finish his story, for they quickly floated to the river's edge, where Christopher Robin and the others were waiting.

"Pooh!" Christopher Robin cried, lifting him off the chair. "Thank goodness you're safe. But where is Piglet?"

All of a sudden something emerged from under the chair. It was Pooh's honeypot!

"H-h-here I am," Piglet replied from inside the pot.

"Pooh!" Christopher Robin cried again. "You rescued Piglet."

"I did?" Pooh said.

"Yes," Christopher Robin said, patting Pooh on the head. "And it was a very brave thing to do. You are a hero!"

"I am?" Pooh said.

"Yes," Christopher Robin said. "And as soon as the flood is over, I shall give you a hero party."

Pooh's hero party had barely begun when Eeyore came trudging in.

"I found a house for Owl," he said.

"I say, Eeyore, good show!" Owl hooted happily. "Where, may I ask, is it?"

"Follow me, and I'll show you," Eeyore said.

So everyone followed Eeyore. But much to their surprise, when they got to Owl's new house, it turned out to be . . .

. . . Piglet's house!

"Why are we stopping here?" Christopher Robin asked.

"This is Owl's new house," Eeyore said proudly. "What do you think of it?"

There was a long moment of silence. Then Christopher Robin said, "It's a nice house, Eeyore, but . . ."

And Kanga said, "It's a lovely house, but . . ."

"It's the best house in the whole world," Piglet sighed, his eyes full of tears.

"Tell them it's your house, Piglet," Pooh whispered.

But Piglet didn't have the heart to disappoint Owl. "No," he said. "This house belongs – *sniff* – to our good friend Owl."

"But Piglet," Rabbit said, "where will *you* live?"

"Well . . . ," Piglet said. "I-I-I guess – *sniff* – I shall l-live . . ."

"With me," Pooh broke in, taking Piglet's hand in his. "You shall live with me, won't you, Piglet?"

"With you?" Piglet said, wiping a tear from his eye. "Oh, thank you, Pooh Bear. Of course I will."

"Piglet, that was a very grand thing to do," Christopher Robin said, taking Piglet's other hand.

"A heroic thing," Rabbit chimed in.

And that's when Pooh had his second good thought in two days. "Christopher Robin," he asked, "can we make a one-hero party into a two-hero party?"

"Of course we can, silly old bear," said Christopher Robin.

And so they did.

Pooh was a hero for saving Piglet, and Piglet was a hero for giving Owl his grand home in the beech tree.

To celebrate these deeds of bravery and generosity, everyone gathered round the heroes, shouting, "Hip, hip, hooray for the Piglet and the Pooh."

Then Pooh and Piglet were scooped up in a blanket and tossed high, high, high into the clear blue sky.

Winnie the Pooh and a Day for Eeyore

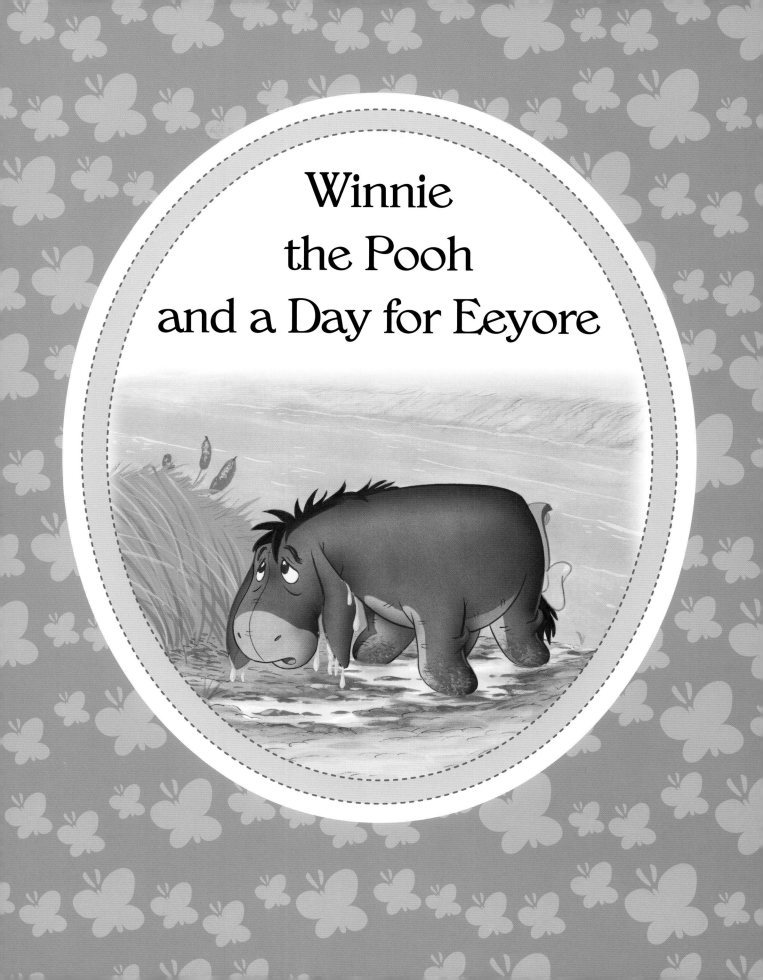

At the edge of the Hundred-Acre Wood, a lovely old bridge crossed a peaceful little river. Now, this bridge was a favourite spot of Winnie the Pooh's, and he would often wander there, doing nothing in particular and thinking nothing in particular. But on one such wandering, something suddenly took Pooh's mind off of nothing. And that something was a big brown pinecone, which dropped – *PLOP!* – right on his head.

Pooh picked up the pinecone and gazed at it thoughtfully. As he walked along, he decided to make up a little poem. But while his head was occupied (he was trying to think of a word that rhymed with *cone*), his feet, left to their own devices, tripped over a tree root, and Pooh tumbled to the ground.

Pooh kept on tumbling until he came to a stop on the bridge, just as the pinecone went skittering over the edge and into the water below.

"Oh bother," said Pooh. "I suppose I shall have to find another one."

Now, Pooh had every intention of doing just that. But the river was slipping away so peacefully beneath him that his thoughts began to slip away with it.

"That's funny," Pooh said to himself as the pinecone drifted under the bridge and floated lazily downstream. "I dropped it on one side, and it came out on the other.

"Hmm . . . ," he murmured, also to himself. "I wonder if it would do that again."

So he collected a rather large and a rather small pinecone and tossed them over the far side of the bridge. Then he scurried to the other side and waited.

"I wonder which one will come out first," said Pooh.

Well, as it turned out, the big one came out first, and the little one came out last, which was just what Pooh had hoped. And that was the beginning of a game called Pooh Sticks, named for its inventor – Winnie the Pooh.

Now, you might think it should have been called Pooh *Cones*, but since it was easier to collect a handful of sticks than an armful of cones, Pooh made a slight improvement on his original game.

And so it came to pass that one fine day Pooh, Piglet, Rabbit
and Roo were all on the bridge playing Pooh Sticks.

"All right now," Rabbit said. "The first stick to pass all the way
under the bridge wins. On your marks, get set, . . . go!"

Pooh, Piglet, Rabbit and Roo all threw their sticks into the
water. Then they raced to the other side of the bridge to see whose
would come out first.

"I can see mine," Roo shouted, pointing to a short black stick in the water. "I win! I win!" he cried, even as the "stick" suddenly spread its wings and flew off to join the other dragonflies flitting about.

"Can you see yours, Pooh?" Piglet asked, peering down at the gently flowing river.

"No," Pooh said. "I expect my stick's stuck."

"They always take longer than you think," Rabbit assured him
just as something long, gray, and quite stick-like floated into view.

"Oh, I can see yours, Piglet," Pooh cried.

"Are you sure it's mine?" Piglet asked doubtfully.

"Sure," said Roo, "it's a grey one. A very big grey one."

"Oh, no, it isn't," said Rabbit. "It's . . . it's . . ."

"Eyore!" everyone shouted.

"Don't pay any attention to me," Eeyore muttered as he floated by his friends, tail first. "Nobody ever does."

Rabbit leaned over the bridge. "Eeyore," he cried. "What are you doing down there?"

"I'll give you three guesses," Eeyore said flatly.

"Fishing?" asked Pooh.

"Wrong," said Eeyore.

"Going for a sail?" Roo guessed.

"Wrong again!"

"Ah, waiting for somebody to help you out of the river?" Rabbit tried.

"That's right," Eeyore mumbled more or less to himself. "Give Rabbit the time and he'll get the answer."

Piglet looked down at his friend in alarm. "Eeyore," he cried,
"what can we . . . I mean, how should we . . . do you think if
we . . ."

"Yes," Eeyore said calmly, "one of those would be just the thing.
Thank you, Piglet."

"I've got an idea," Pooh offered hesitantly. "But I don't suppose
it's a very good one."

"I don't suppose it is," Eeyore gurgled as his head tipped
beneath the water.

"Go on, Pooh," Rabbit urged. "Let's have it."

"Well," Pooh said, "if we all threw stones and things into the river on one side of Eeyore, the stones would make waves, and the waves would wash him to the other side."

"That's a fine idea," said Rabbit. "I'm glad we thought of it, Pooh." But Pooh had already gone off to find a suitable stone.

Eeyore floated around and around in a circle until finally Pooh reappeared, rolling a great big boulder onto the bridge.

Rabbit immediately took charge. "Piglet," he directed, "give Pooh a little more room. Roo, get back a bit." And to Pooh he said, "I think a little to the left. No, no, a little to the right."

It took a while, but Pooh finally got the stone lined up to Rabbit's satisfaction. "Pooh," Rabbit said then, "when I say 'Now,' you can drop it."

Then he turned to Eeyore and said, "When I say 'Now,' Pooh
will drop the stone. Are you ready . . . ?"

"One . . . ," Rabbit counted. "Two . . . ," and, "now!" he cried.

And with that, Pooh gave a mighty heave that sent the boulder
off the bridge – and right smack on top of Eeyore!

"Oh dear," Pooh sighed as Eeyore sank out of sight. "Perhaps it
wasn't such a very good idea after all."

Pooh was still peering woefully at the spot where his friend had
disappeared when Eeyore came sloshing out of the water and onto
the riverbank.

"Oh, Eeyore," Piglet squealed. "You're all wet."

"That happens when you've been in a river a long time,"
Eeyore said, shaking himself dry and giving Piglet a bit of a
bath in the process.

"How did you fall in the river, Eeyore?" Rabbit asked.

"I didn't *fall* in," Eeyore said. "I was *bounced* in! I was just sitting by the side of the river, minding my own business, when I received a loud bounce."

"But who did it?" Pooh wanted to know.

"I expect it was T-Tigger," Piglet replied.

The words were no sooner out of Piglet's mouth than Tigger himself bounced onto the scene and knocked Rabbit flat on his back!

"Eeyore," Rabbit said, scrambling to his feet, "was it Tigger who bounced you?"

"I didn't bounce him," said Tigger. "I happened to be behind Eeyore and I . . . I simply coughed."

"You bounced me," Eeyore said accusingly.

"I didn't bounce," Tigger repeated. "I coughed."

"Bouncing or coughing," Eeyore said, "it's all the same."

"Oh no, it's not," Tigger insisted.

But after several more rounds of "Bounced!" "Coughed!" "Did not!" "Did too!" Tigger finally admitted that he had in fact bounced Eeyore into the water.

"It was just a joke," he said sheepishly. But no one was laughing, least of all Eeyore.

"Some people have no sense of humour," Tigger grumbled as he went bouncing off into the woods.

"Tigger is so thoughtless," Rabbit said.

"Why should Tigger think of me?" Eeyore said. "No one else does."

"Why do you say that, Eeyore?" Pooh asked, but Eeyore was already shambling away, head hung, shoulders drooping.

Eeyore followed the stream back to his Gloomy Spot. As he sat there under what seemed to be his very own rain cloud, he could see his sad face in the water. "Pathetic," Eeyore said to his reflection.

Eeyore lumbered around to the other side of the bank and peered into the water again. "Just as I thought," he said. "No better from here. Pa-thetic," he repeated.

At the sound of footsteps, Eeyore looked up. And there was his friend Pooh.

"Eeyore," Pooh said softly. "What's the matter?"

"What makes you think anything's the matter?" Eeyore sighed.

"You seem so sad," said Pooh.

"Why should I be sad?" Eeyore asked sadly. And then, answering his own question, he said, "It's my birthday. The happiest day of the year."

"Your birthday?" Pooh said, surprised.

"Of course," Eeyore said. "Can't you see the presents?"

"No," Pooh replied, looking around in confusion.

"Can't you see the cake?" Eeyore went on. "The candles and the pink icing?"

"Well, no," Pooh said, more confused than before.

"Neither can I," Eeyore said with a sigh.

"Oh," said Pooh. Not quite sure what to say next, he said, "Well, many happy returns of the day, Eeyore."

"Thank you, Pooh," Eeyore said. "But we can't all . . . And some of us don't."

"Can't all what?" Pooh asked.

"No gaiety," Eeyore intoned. "No song and dance. No 'Here We Go Round the Mulberry Bush.' But don't worry about me, Pooh," he said. "Go and enjoy yourself. I'll stay here and be miserable, with no presents, no cake and no candles. . . ."

As Eeyore's mournful voice trailed off, Pooh gently patted him on the back and said, "Eeyore, wait right here." Then he hurried off as fast as he could.

When Pooh got home, he found Piglet jumping up and down at the door, trying desperately to reach the door knocker.

"Here, let me do it," said Pooh, lifting the knocker.

"B-but Pooh –" Piglet started.

"I found out what's troubling Eeyore," Pooh interrupted. "It's his birthday, and nobody has taken any notice of it."

Pooh looked at the still-closed door. "Well, whoever lives here certainly takes a long time to answer the door."

"But Pooh, isn't this . . . your house?" asked Piglet.

"Oh, so it is," answered Pooh.

As the two friends went inside, Pooh declared, "I must get poor Eeyore a present. But what?" he wondered, looking around for a likely gift.

Just then Pooh spied a small honeypot in the pantry. "Ah, honey," he cried. "That should do very well." And turning to Piglet, he said, "What are you giving Eeyore?"

For a moment poor Piglet seemed quite at a loss, but then he said, "Perhaps I could give Eeyore a balloon."

"That," said Pooh, "is a very good idea!"

"I have one at home," Piglet exclaimed. "I'll go and get it right now."

So off Piglet hurried in one direction, and off Pooh went in the other.

Pooh hadn't gone far when a funny
feeling crept over him. It began at the
very tip of his nose and trickled all
the way down to his toes. It was as if
someone inside him were saying, "Now
then, Pooh, time for a little something."

So Pooh reached into the honeypot
and had a little something. Then he had
a little more, and still a little more. And
before long he had licked the honeypot
clean.

As Pooh absentmindedly wiped the
last sticky drop from his mouth, he said,
"Now, where was I going? Oh yes,
Eeyore. I was . . ." And looking down at
the empty jar he said, "Oh bother, I must
give Eeyore something."

But first, Pooh decided, he'd go visit
his good friend Owl.

Owl was busy hanging a picture of his great-uncle Robert on the wall when Pooh knocked at the door.

"Many happy returns of Eeyore's birthday," Pooh said.

"You know, that reminds me of a birthday of my great-uncle Robert," Owl said, waving Pooh in with one wing and pointing to the newly hung portrait with the other.

"Uncle Robert had just reached the ripe old age of one hundred and three," Owl explained, "though of course he would only admit to ninety-seven. We all felt that a celebration was in order, so . . ."

"What are you giving him?" Pooh broke in the moment Owl paused for breath.

"Giving who?" Owl asked, peering quizzically at Pooh.

"Eeyore," Pooh replied.

"Oh, Eeyore," Owl chuckled. "Of course! I, ah . . . Well, what are *you* giving him, Pooh?"

"I'm giving him this useful pot to keep things in," said Pooh, holding out the empty honeypot, "and I—"

"A useful pot?" said Owl, peering into the jar. "Evidently someone has been keeping honey in it."

"Yes," said Pooh. "It's very useful like that, but I wanted to ask you—"

"You ought to write 'Happy Birthday' on it," said Owl.

"That was what I wanted to ask you," explained Pooh. "My own spelling is a bit wobbly."

"Very well," Owl said. And he took the pot and his pen and got down to work. "It's easier if people don't look while I'm writing," he added, turning his back on Pooh.

After what seemed a rather long time, Owl turned around again.

"There!" he said, proudly holding up the pot. "All finished. What do you think of it?"

"It looks like a lot of words just to say 'Happy Birthday,'" Pooh pointed out.

"Well, actually, I wrote 'A Very Happy Birthday, with Love from Pooh,'" Owl explained. "Naturally it takes a good deal of words to say something like that."

"Oh, I see," Pooh said, taking the pot. "Thank you, Owl."

While Pooh went to deliver his gift to Eeyore, Owl headed off to Christopher Robin's house. On the way, he flew directly over Piglet, who was running along with a big red balloon.

"Many happy returns of Eeyore's birthday, Piglet," Owl hollered down.

"Many happy returns to you, too, Owl," Piglet hollered up.

But as Piglet hollered up, he neglected to look down and ran smack into a tree.

Piglet bounced off the tree and came to a stop – *POP!* – right on top of what *had been* the big red balloon.

"Oh d-d-dear. How shall I . . . ? What shall I . . . ? Well . . . maybe Eeyore doesn't like balloons so very much," Piglet said.

So he trudged off to Eeyore's, dragging the remains of the balloon behind him. Piglet found his friend moping under a leafless tree.

"Many happy returns of the day," Piglet sang out.

"Meaning my birthday," Eeyore said glumly.

"Yes," said Piglet. "And I've brought you a present."

"Pardon me, Piglet," Eeyore said, perking up. "My hearing must be going. I thought you said you brought me a present."

"I did," said Piglet. "I brought you a b-balloon."

"Balloon?" Eeyore echoed, his ears pricking up. "Did you say 'balloon'?"

"Yes," Piglet said. "But I'm afraid, I'm very sorry, but when I was running, that is, to bring it, I . . . I . . ."

Piglet's words wound down as he held out what was left of Eeyore's birthday balloon.

Eeyore took one look and said, "Red. My favourite colour. How big was it?" he couldn't help asking.

"About as big as m-me," Piglet replied.

"My favourite size," Eeyore said wistfully.

Eeyore was sadly eyeing the shredded red balloon when
Pooh appeared. "I've brought you a little present, Eeyore," he
announced. "It's a useful pot. It's got 'A Very Happy Birthday,
with Love from Pooh' written on it. And it's for putting things in."

"Like a balloon?" Eeyore said hopefully.

"Oh, no. Balloons are much too big . . . ," Pooh began, even as
Eeyore picked the balloon up with his teeth and dropped it into the
very useful pot.

"It *does* fit!" Pooh marvelled as Eeyore carefully pulled the balloon out of the pot, then dropped it back in again.

"Eeyore, I'm very glad I thought of giving you a useful pot to put things in," said Pooh.

"And I'm very glad I thought of giving you something to put in a useful pot," said Piglet.

Eeyore didn't say anything. But he looked very, very glad.

It was then that Christopher Robin arrived, along with Owl, Kanga, Roo, Rabbit and a lovely chocolate birthday cake!

After his friends all sang "Happy Birthday," Eeyore made a wish and blew out the candles. Then Owl clapped his wings and cried, "Bravo! Good show! This reminds me of the party we once gave for my great-uncle Robert. . . ."

Owl had barely begun his story when he was interrupted by a cheerful "Halloo!"

"Oh no! Oh no! Oh no!" cried Rabbit just as Tigger bounced right into him and knocked him to the ground.

"Hello, Tigger," said Roo. "We're having a party."

"A party!" cried Tigger. "Oh boy, oh boy, oh boy. Tiggers love parties." And with no further ado, he bounced over to the table and gobbled up a fistful of cake.

"You've got a lot of nerve showing up here after what you did to Eeyore," Rabbit scolded Tigger. "I think you should leave now."

"Aw, let him stay," cried Roo.

"What do you think, Christopher Robin?" Pooh asked.

"I think," said Christopher Robin, "we all ought to play Pooh Sticks."

And that's exactly what they did.

Eeyore, who had never played the game before, won more times than anybody else. But poor Tigger didn't win at all.

When it was time for everyone to go home, Tigger threw down his stick and grumbled, "Tiggers don't like Pooh Sticks!" Then, instead of going off in his usual bouncy way, he walked off with his head down and no bounce at all.

"I'd be happy to tell you my secret for winning at Pooh Sticks," Eeyore said, hurrying after Tigger. "It's easy. You just have to let your stick drop in a twitchy sort of way."

"Oh yeah," said Tigger, brightening up immediately. "I forgot to twitch. That was my problem." And then, just because he was feeling so happy, he began bouncing again.

And of course he bounced right into Eeyore.

Meanwhile, Pooh, Piglet and Christopher Robin lingered on the bridge, quietly watching the peaceful stream.

At last Piglet said, "Tigger's all right, really."

"Of course he is," Christopher Robin agreed.

"Everybody is, really," Pooh mused. "That's what I think." He hesitated a moment, then added, "But I don't suppose I'm right."

"Of course you are," said Christopher Robin, patting Pooh's head. "Silly old bear."